W9-DIN-324

SUMMER CAMP SCIENCE MYSTERIES

#6 The Whispering Lake Ghosts

A Mystery about Sound

by Lynda Beauregard

illustrated by German Torres

GRAPHIC UNIVERSE™ • MINNEAPOLIS • NEW YORK

Angie Rayez

Alex Rayez

Jordan Collins

Braelin Walker

Megan Taylor

Carly Livingston

DON'T MISS THE EXPERIMENTS ON PAGES 45 AND 46!

MYSTERIOUS WORDS AND MORE ON PAGE 47!

Kyle Reed

Loraine Sanders

J.D. Hamilton

Sound is a vibration that moves in waves.

The distance it travels and the speed at which it travels depend on the type of matter (stuff) it is moving through. As sound waves travel farther, they disperse and lose energy, making them harder to hear. Sound waves also bounce off hard objects such as walls.

How high or low a sound is depends on the pitch, or frequency of the sound wave. The human ear can only hear a certain range of frequencies—some are too high or low for humans to hear.

Story by Lynda Beauregard
Art by German Torres
Coloring by John Novak
Lettering by Grace Lu

Graphic Universe™
A division of Lerner Publishing Group, Inc.
241 First Avenue North
Minneapolis, MN 55401 U.S.A.

Website address: www.lernerbooks.com

Main body text set in CCWildwords.
Typeface provided by Comicraft/Active Images.

Library of Congress Cataloging-in-Publication Data

Beauregard, Lynda.
    The whispering lake ghosts : a mystery about sound / by Lynda Beauregard ; illustrated by German Torres. — 1st American ed.
        p.   cm. — (Summer camp science mysteries ; #6)
        Summary: Hearing strange murmuring near the lake, campers Braelin and Megan search for the ghostly voices, putting their new knowledge of sound and amplification to good use.
        ISBN 978–1–4677–0168–6 (lib. bdg. : alk. paper)
        1. Graphic novels. [1. Graphic novels. 2. Camps—Fiction. 3. Sound—Fiction.]
I. Torres, German, ill. II. Title.
PZ7.7.B42Wh 2013
741.5i973—dc23   2012017722

Manufactured in the United States of America
1 – CG – 12/31/12

COME ON, BRAELIN! I'M STARVING!

I'M HUNGRY TOO, BUT...

YIPE!

IT'S JUST THUNDER, BRAELIN. IT WON'T HURT YOU.

NO, BUT THE LIGHTNING COULD!

THE LIGHTNING IS PROBABLY TOO FAR AWAY.

I THINK THERE'S A WAY YOU CAN TELL, BY COUNTING THE SECONDS BETWEEN THE FLASH AND THE SOUND.

ONE ONE THOUSAND, TWO ONE THOUSAND, THREE ONE THOUSAND, FOUR ONE THOUSAND, FIVE ONE THOUSAND...

SIX ONE THOUSAND...

BOOM!

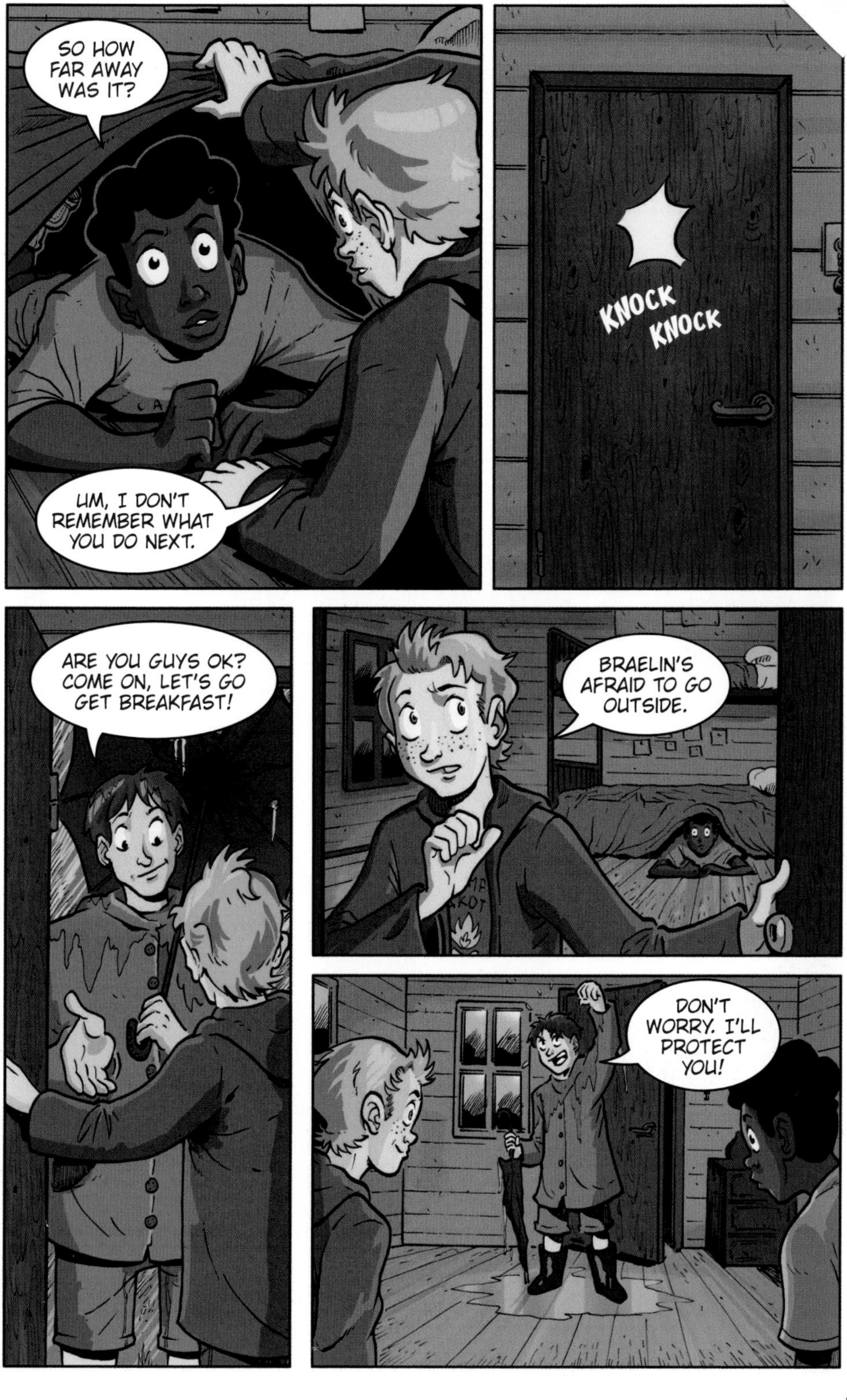
SO HOW FAR AWAY WAS IT?
UM, I DON'T REMEMBER WHAT YOU DO NEXT.
KNOCK KNOCK
ARE YOU GUYS OK? COME ON, LET'S GO GET BREAKFAST!
BRAELIN'S AFRAID TO GO OUTSIDE.
DON'T WORRY. I'LL PROTECT YOU!

IT'S OK, BRAELIN. LET'S HURRY UP AND GET INSIDE THE MAIN CABIN.

BOOM!

I TRIED TO HELP HIM FIGURE OUT HOW FAR AWAY THE LIGHTNING WAS, BUT I COULDN'T REMEMBER HOW TO DO IT.

YOU HAVE TO DO SOME CALCULATIONS. I'LL SHOW YOU WHEN WE GET INSIDE.

BRAELIN! YOU MADE IT!

OK, SO WE KNOW THE SPEED OF SOUND IS ABOUT 1,125 FEET PER SECOND.

WE DO?

OK, WAIT FOR THE LIGHTNING. THEN START COUNTING THE SECONDS.

ONE ONE THOUSAND, TWO ONE THOUSAND, THREE ONE THOUSAND, FOUR ONE THOUSAND...

FIVE ONE THOUSAND--

BOOM!

IT TOOK FIVE SECONDS FOR THE SOUND TO GET HERE.

MULTIPLY THE SPEED OF SOUND BY THE TIME...

$$\overset{1\ 2}{1125} \times 5 = 5625$$

THAT MAKES 5,625 FEET. NOW, WHO CAN TELL ME HOW MANY FEET IN A MILE?

5,000-SOMETHING?

5,280 FEET.

WHOA.

RIGHT, CARLY! THAT MEANS THE LIGHTNING WAS A LITTLE MORE THAN A MILE AWAY.

ONLY A MILE AWAY?

WELL, IT'S PROBABLY MORE THAN THAT. THE SPEED OF SOUND CHANGES, DEPENDING ON WHAT THE SOUND IS TRAVELING THROUGH.

SOUND TRAVELS FASTER IN WATER THAN IT DOES IN AIR, AND WE HAVE A LOT OF WATER IN THE AIR RIGHT NOW!

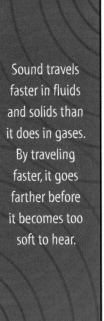

Sound travels faster in fluids and solids than it does in gases. By traveling faster, it goes farther before it becomes too soft to hear.

I THINK YOU NEED A NEW UMBRELLA, KYLE.

DON'T THROW IT AWAY! I THINK I CAN USE IT FOR SOMETHING.

I JUST WISH THE THUNDER WASN'T SO LOUD.

I PRETEND THE THUNDER AND LIGHTNING ARE FIREWORKS.

ACTUALLY, THEY'RE A LOT ALIKE, ANGIE.

THEY ARE?

SURE. BOTH LIGHTNING BOLTS AND FIREWORKS EXPLOSIONS CHANGE THE AIR PRESSURE AROUND THEM, PUSHING THE AIR OUTWARD.

Lightning bolts generate heat. The heat compresses the surrounding air. This makes an area of low air pressure surrounded by higher air pressure.

THE RAPID EXPANSION AND CONTRACTION OF AIR MAKES A SOUND WAVE. THAT'S THUNDER!

MY BROTHER TOLD ME IT WAS FROM THE BOWLING BALL HITTING THE PINS.

HUH?

WHAT ARE YOU TALKING ABOUT, BRAELIN?

YOU KNOW, WHEN GIANTS GO BOWLING.

THERE'S NO SUCH THING AS GIANTS!

I SUPPOSE THERE'S NO SUCH THING AS *LAKE GHOSTS*, EITHER?

LAKE GHOSTS?

UH-HUH. SOMETIMES, WHEN YOU'RE DOWN BY THE LAKE, YOU CAN HEAR THEM.

THEY'RE TALKING, BUT YOU CAN'T QUITE HEAR WHAT THEY'RE SAYING.

AND IF YOU LOOK AROUND, THERE'S NO ONE THERE.

YOU'RE MAKING THIS UP!

NO, I'VE HEARD THEM TOO.

NO WAY. LORAINE, ARE THERE REALLY LAKE GHOSTS?

I DON'T KNOW ABOUT GHOSTS, BUT I HAVE HEARD VOICES DOWN BY THE WATER.

OK, EVERYONE, FINISH UP SO WE CAN START WORKING ON OUR CRAFT PROJECT!

WHAT ARE WE MAKING?

FLUTES!

START WITH A CARDBOARD TUBE FROM A ROLL OF WRAPPING PAPER THAT'S TRIMMED DOWN SO IT'S 12 INCHES LONG.

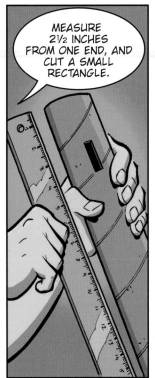

MEASURE 2½ INCHES FROM ONE END, AND CUT A SMALL RECTANGLE.

THAT WILL BE THE MOUTHPIECE OF YOUR FLUTE.

NEXT, MEASURE 5 INCHES FROM THE END OF YOUR FLUTE, AND MAKE 5 HOLES IN A LINE, EACH ABOUT 1 INCH APART.

IT SHOULD LOOK LIKE THIS.

THEN WE'LL COVER THE TOP OF OUR FLUTE, THE OPEN END NEAR THE MOUTHPIECE, WITH PLASTIC TAPE.

THEN THE AIR CAN'T ESCAPE THROUGH THAT END WHEN YOU BLOW THROUGH THE MOUTHPIECE.

NOW FOR THE FUN PART--LET'S DECORATE OUR FLUTES!

AND WHILE YOU'RE DOING THAT, I'LL TELL YOU THE STORY ABOUT THE VERY FIRST FLUTE!

LORAINE IS ALMOST AS FAMOUS FOR STORIES AS SHE IS FOR TRICKS!

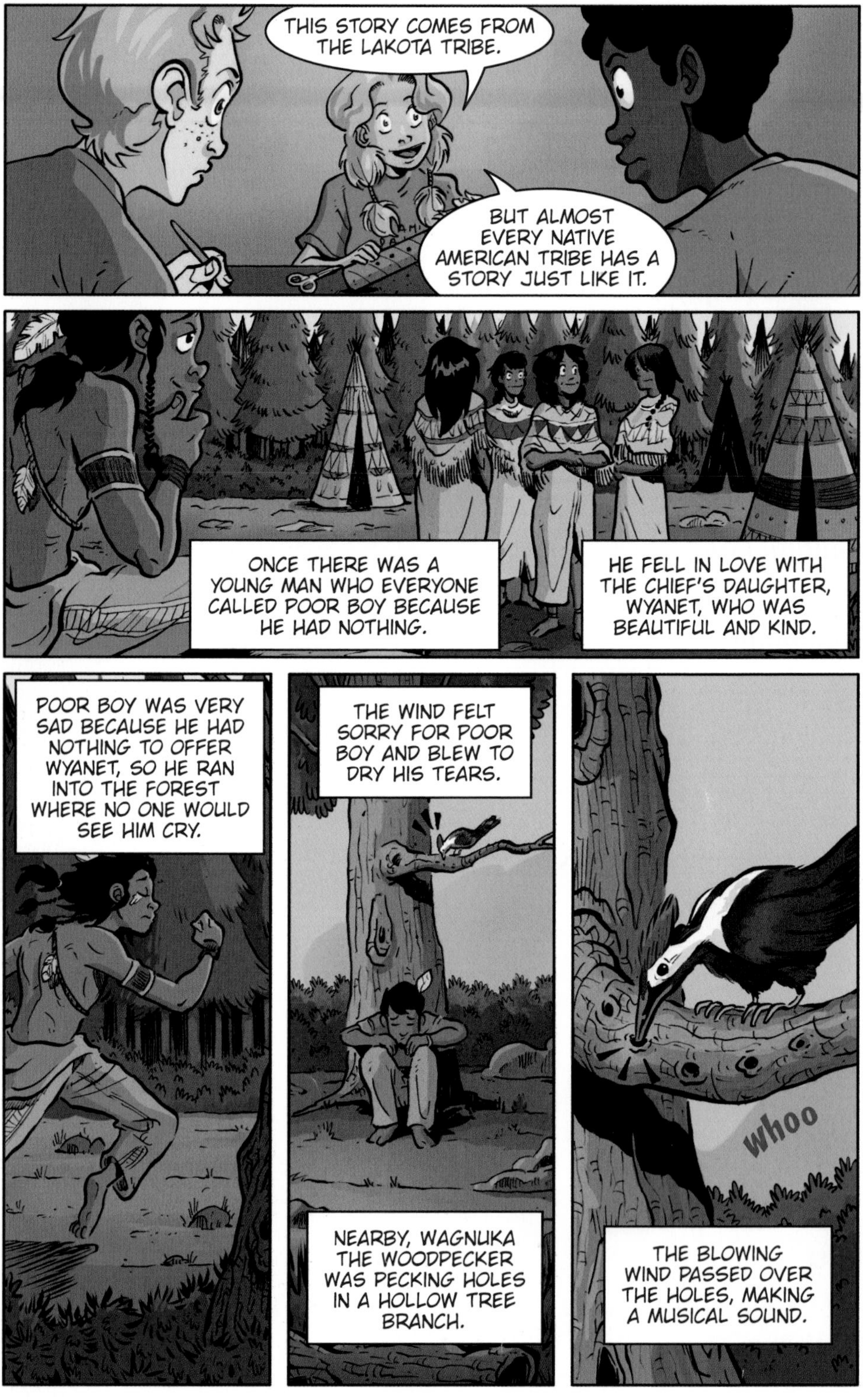
THIS STORY COMES FROM THE LAKOTA TRIBE.
BUT ALMOST EVERY NATIVE AMERICAN TRIBE HAS A STORY JUST LIKE IT.
ONCE THERE WAS A YOUNG MAN WHO EVERYONE CALLED POOR BOY BECAUSE HE HAD NOTHING.
HE FELL IN LOVE WITH THE CHIEF'S DAUGHTER, WYANET, WHO WAS BEAUTIFUL AND KIND.
POOR BOY WAS VERY SAD BECAUSE HE HAD NOTHING TO OFFER WYANET, SO HE RAN INTO THE FOREST WHERE NO ONE WOULD SEE HIM CRY.
THE WIND FELT SORRY FOR POOR BOY AND BLEW TO DRY HIS TEARS.
NEARBY, WAGNUKA THE WOODPECKER WAS PECKING HOLES IN A HOLLOW TREE BRANCH.
whoo
THE BLOWING WIND PASSED OVER THE HOLES, MAKING A MUSICAL SOUND.

SUDDENLY, THE BRANCH BROKE FROM THE TREE AND FELL TO THE GROUND.

IT WAS A GIFT FROM THE WIND AND WAGNUKA.

POOR BOY PICKED UP THE BRANCH AND HEADED HOME. ALONG THE WAY, HE SPOTTED A BULL ELK.

THE ELK WAS SINGING A LOVE SONG TO HIS COWS. POOR BOY DID HIS BEST TO COPY THE SONG ON HIS FLUTE.

AFTER HE GOT HOME, POOR BOY HID BY THE STREAM AND WAITED FOR WYANET. WHEN SHE CAME TO GET WATER FOR COOKING, HE PLAYED THE ELK'S LOVE SONG ON HIS FLUTE.

WYANET WAS ENCHANTED BY POOR BOY'S SONG. HE OFFERED HER THE SONG AND HIS HEART, AND SHE ACCEPTED.

AFTER THAT, POOR BOY WAS KNOWN AS FLUTE BOY AND NEVER HUNTED ELK AGAIN.

DID FLUTE BOY AND WYANET KISS?

EWWW!

CAN ANYONE GUESS WHY NATIVE AMERICAN FLUTES OFTEN HAVE A CARVED BIRD ON THE TOP?

TO THANK THE WOODPECKER FOR GIVING THE FLUTE TO THE PEOPLE?

EXACTLY!

BUT HOW DOES AIR MOVING THROUGH A HOLLOW BRANCH OR A FLUTE MAKE MUSIC?

THE AIR VIBRATES INSIDE THE FLUTE, WHICH MAKES A SOUND. COVERING THE HOLES CHANGES WHERE THE VIBRATING AIR COMES OUT.

The flute's shape makes a vibrating column of air. As this column travels, the vibrations slow down. As the vibrations get slower, they make a lower sound.

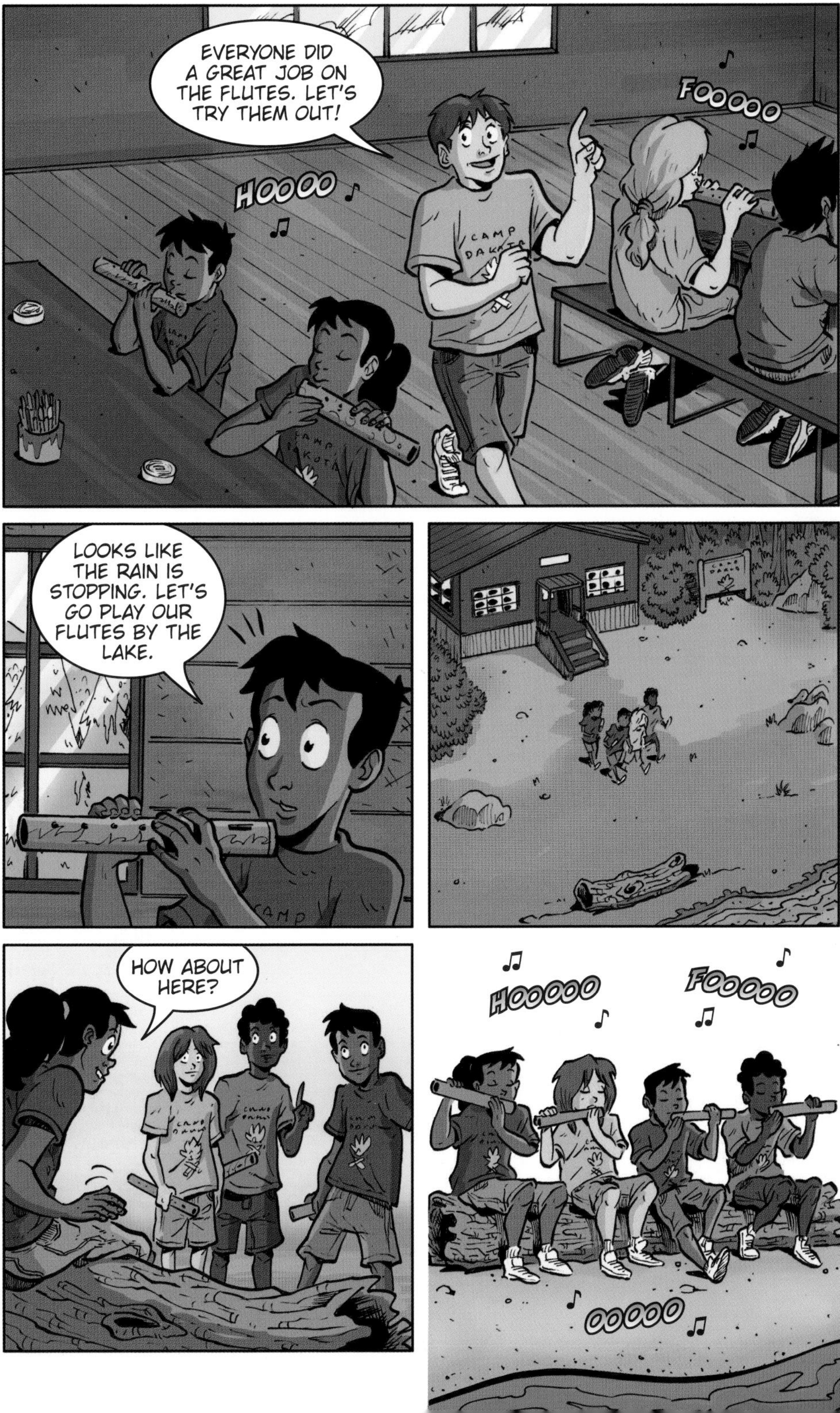
EVERYONE DID A GREAT JOB ON THE FLUTES. LET'S TRY THEM OUT!
FOOOOO
HOOOO
LOOKS LIKE THE RAIN IS STOPPING. LET'S GO PLAY OUR FLUTES BY THE LAKE.
HOW ABOUT HERE?
HOOOOO
FOOOOO
OOOOO

WHAT'S THAT?

mmrmur mmrmur

ARE THOSE VOICES COMING FROM THE MAIN CABIN?

NO, THEY'RE COMING FROM THE LAKE...

LAKE GHOSTS!

MEANWHILE...

WHAT IS THAT?

HM? OH, THAT'S AN OLD RECORDER.

WHAT ARE YOU DOING WITH IT?

I'M GOING TO USE IT FOR AN EXPERIMENT. I THINK I CAN USE THIS UMBRELLA TO AMPLIFY SOUNDS.

REALLY? HOW?

LAKE GHOSTS! LAKE GHOSTS!

YOU SAW GHOSTS?

NO, BUT WE HEARD THEM!

LET'S GO CHECK IT OUT.

I'M STAYING HERE. IT'S STILL TOO WET OUT THERE.

LISTEN!

I DON'T HEAR ANYTHING.

MAYBE THE GHOSTS ARE AFRAID OF ME.

YOU *ARE* PRETTY SCARY.

LET'S GO SEE WHAT ELSE WE CAN HEAR.

WHERE DO YOU THINK WE MIGHT FIND SOME INTERESTING SOUNDS?

THE STABLE, MAYBE?

I WANT TO GO SWIMMING.

IT'S A LITTLE TOO COLD FOR SWIMMING TODAY-- WHICH MEANS I HAVE SOME FREE TIME!

I'M GOING TO TRY OUT MY NEW FISH FINDER. WANT TO HELP?

SURE!

SO HOW DOES IT FIND FISH?

IT USES SONAR.

WHAT'S THAT?

IT'S LIKE THE ECHOLOCATION THAT BATS USE. IT SENDS SOUND WAVES INTO THE WATER.

WHEN THEY HIT SOMETHING, THEY BOUNCE BACK.

THIS THING IS SO SMART, IT CAN TELL HOW BIG AND HOW FAR DOWN THE FISH ARE, JUST BY HOW LONG IT TAKES FOR THE SOUND WAVES TO BOUNCE BACK.

SO WHERE ARE ALL THE FISH?

NOT HERE, APPARENTLY. I JUST SEE ONE.

OK, LET'S SEE WHAT WE'VE GOT.

Neeeeighh

I CAN BARELY HEAR IT.

I KNOW. THE MICROPHONE ISN'T PICKING UP ENOUGH SOUND WAVES. LET'S SEE WHAT WE CAN DO WITH THIS.

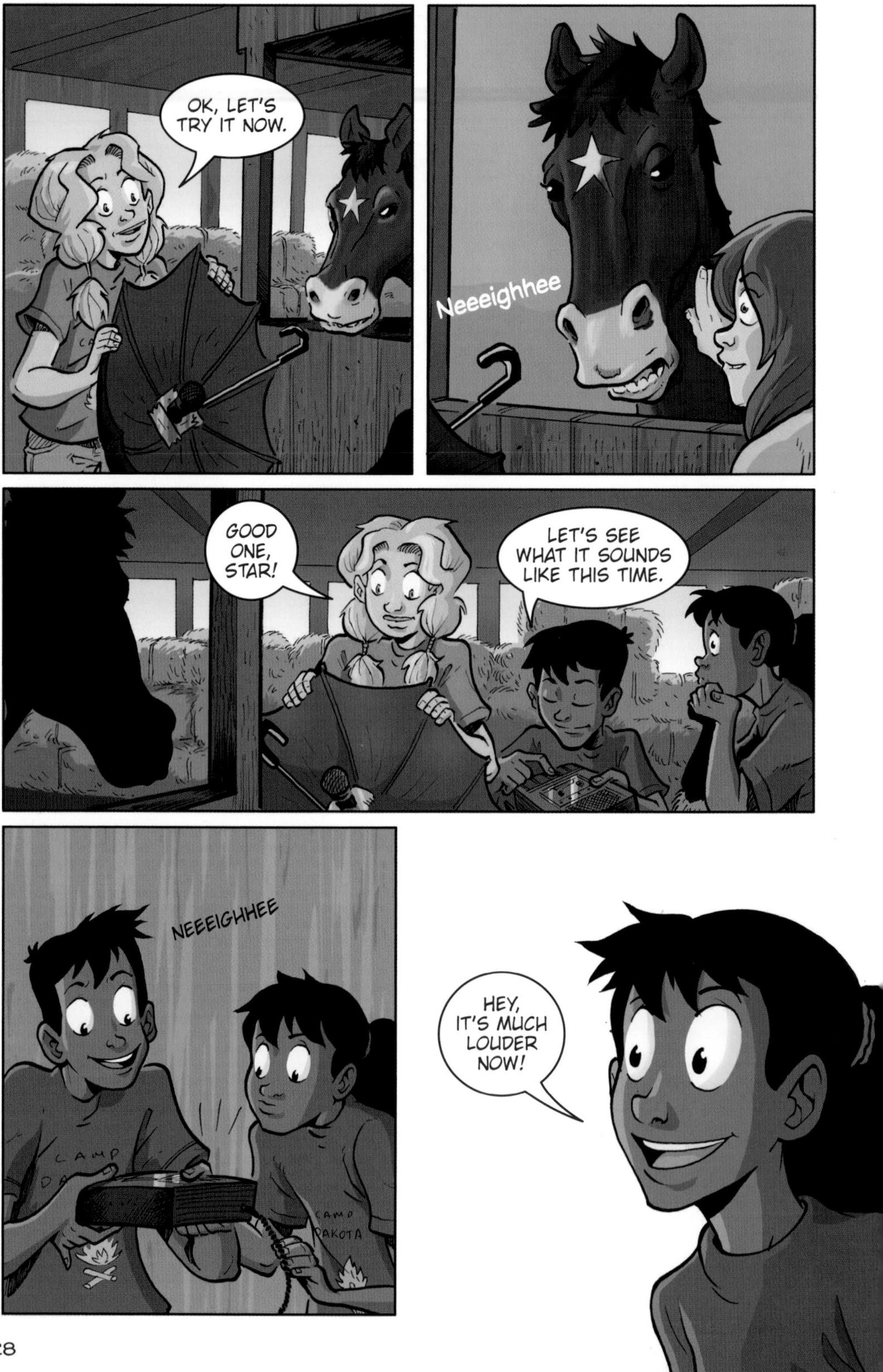
OK, LET'S TRY IT NOW.
Neeeighhee
GOOD ONE, STAR!
LET'S SEE WHAT IT SOUNDS LIKE THIS TIME.
NEEEIGHHEE
CAMP DAKOTA
HEY, IT'S MUCH LOUDER NOW!

THAT'S BECAUSE THE CONE SHAPE OF THE UMBRELLA HELPED COLLECT AND CONCENTRATE THE SOUND WAVES, SO MORE OF THEM WERE PICKED UP BY THE MICROPHONE.

Cone shaped amplifiers can also work the opposite way too, making sound coming out of speakers and megaphones louder.

SHALL WE FIND SOME OTHER SOUNDS TO RECORD?

LET'S GO!

♪ ♫

HEY, GUYS, WHERE HAVE YOU BEEN?

WE TRIED OUT J.D.'S FISH FINDER.

BUT WE ONLY FOUND ONE FISH.

WE'VE BEEN USING KYLE'S BEAT-UP UMBRELLA TO MAKE QUIET SOUNDS LOUDER.

LOOKS LIKE IT MAY RAIN AGAIN SOON. WE'D BETTER GET BACK TO THE MAIN CABIN.

HEY, LORAINE, CAN I BORROW THAT?

I SUPPOSE SO. JUST DON'T STAY OUT HERE VERY LONG. I DON'T LIKE THE LOOK OF THOSE CLOUDS.

WHAT ARE YOU GOING TO DO WITH IT?

RECORD THE GHOST VOICES SO I CAN TELL WHAT THEY'RE SAYING.

YOU KNOW HOW TO WORK THIS?

YOU BET!

NOPE. NOTHING.

I'M NOT GIVING UP. LET'S TRY AGAIN, OVER THERE.

MAYBE THE GHOSTS HAVE MOVED TO THE FOREST. COME ON, MEGAN.

I DON'T THINK WE SHOULD...

IT'LL BE FINE.

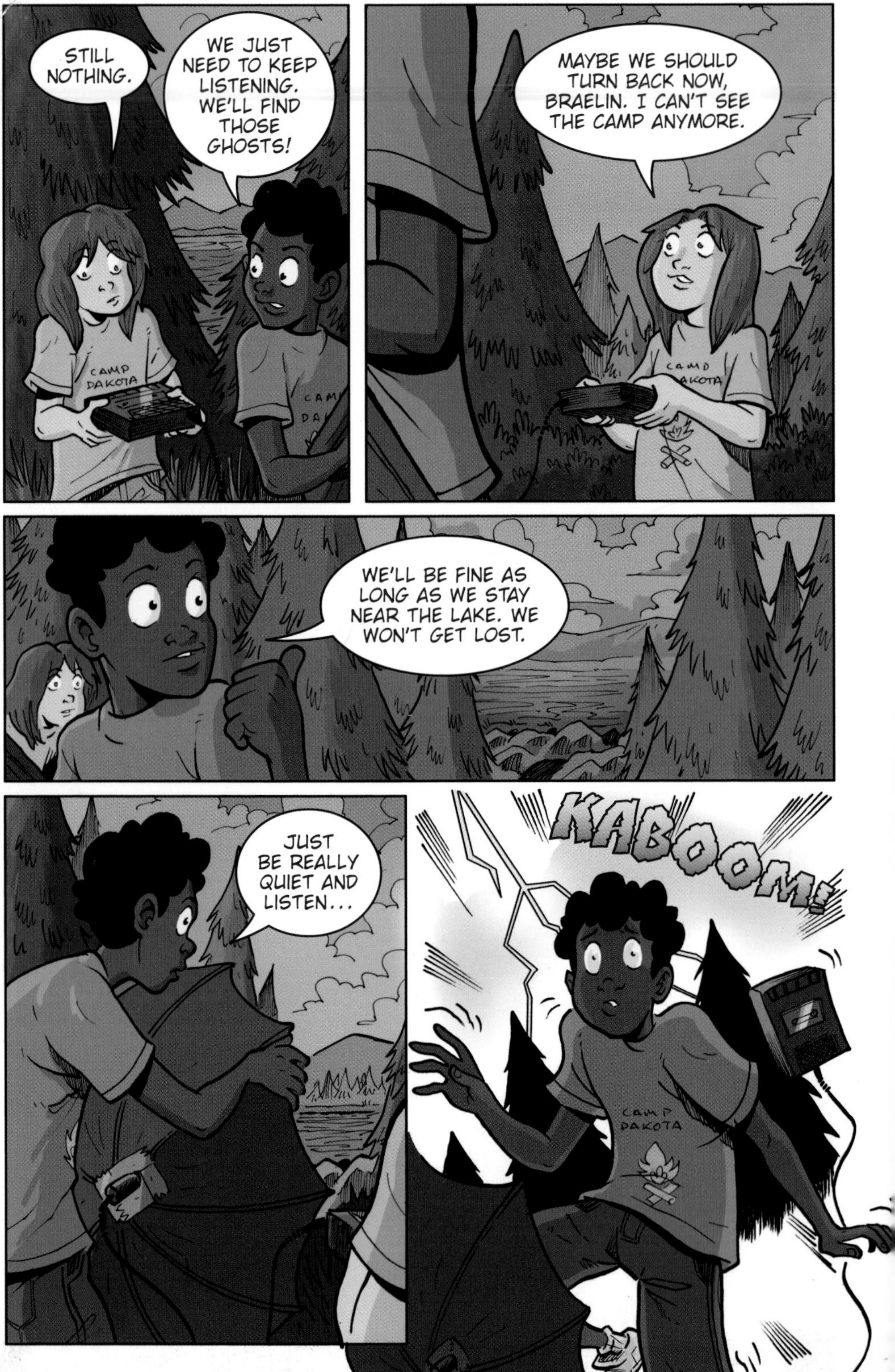
STILL NOTHING.
WE JUST NEED TO KEEP LISTENING. WE'LL FIND THOSE GHOSTS!
CAMP DAKOTA
MAYBE WE SHOULD TURN BACK NOW, BRAELIN. I CAN'T SEE THE CAMP ANYMORE.
CAMP DAKOTA
WE'LL BE FINE AS LONG AS WE STAY NEAR THE LAKE. WE WON'T GET LOST.
JUST BE REALLY QUIET AND LISTEN...
KABOOOM!
CAMP DAKOTA

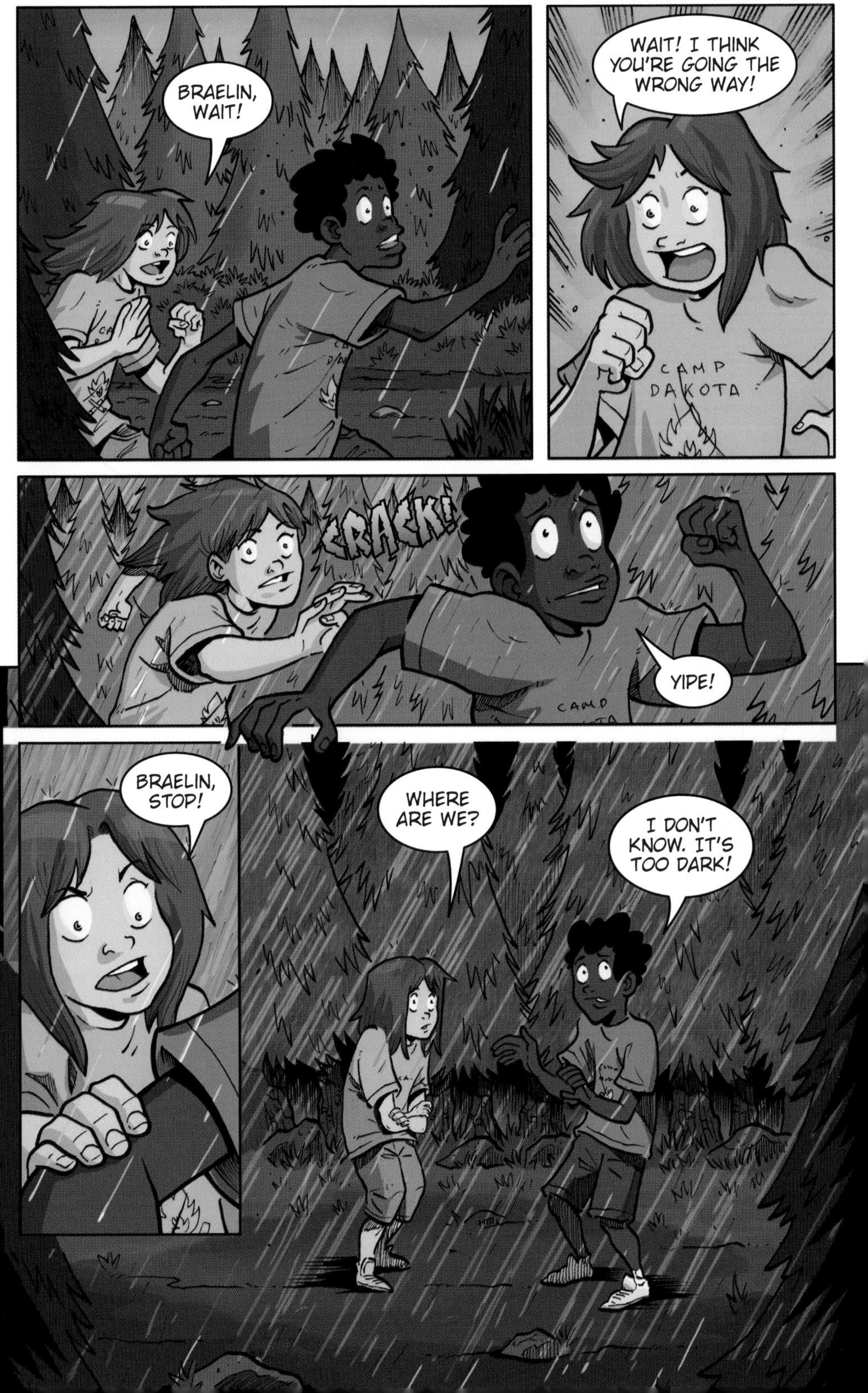
BRAELIN, WAIT!
WAIT! I THINK YOU'RE GOING THE WRONG WAY!
CAMP DAKOTA
CRACK!
YIPE!
BRAELIN, STOP!
WHERE ARE WE?
I DON'T KNOW. IT'S TOO DARK!

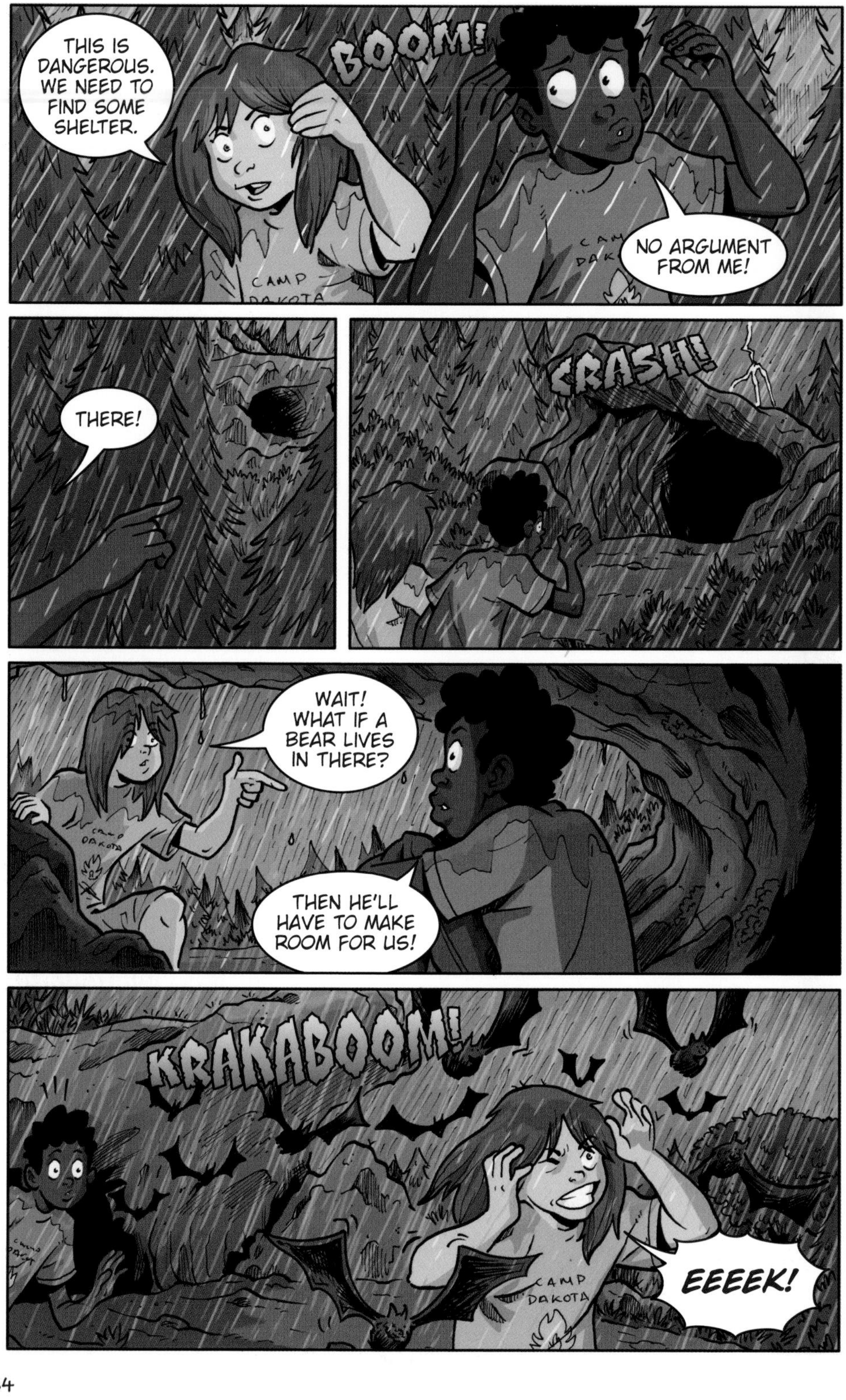
THIS IS DANGEROUS. WE NEED TO FIND SOME SHELTER.
BOOM!
NO ARGUMENT FROM ME!
CAMP DAKOTA
THERE!
CRASH!
WAIT! WHAT IF A BEAR LIVES IN THERE?
THEN HE'LL HAVE TO MAKE ROOM FOR US!
KRAKABOOM!
EEEEK!
CAMP DAKOTA

I AM **NOT** GOING IN THERE!

COME ON! LIGHTNING IS WORSE THAN BATS!

NOT IF ONE GETS STUCK IN MY HAIR!

BATS WON'T HIT YOU. THEY KNOW WHERE YOU ARE, EVEN IN THE DARK.

HOW?

THEY USE ECHO-SOMETHING... ECHOLOCATION!

IT WORKS LIKE J.D.'S FISH FINDER. BATS MAKE A SOUND WAVE, THEN LISTEN CAREFULLY FOR THE ECHO AS IT BOUNCES OFF SOMETHING. THE ECHO TELLS THEM WHERE THINGS ARE.

The sound wave that bats produce is at too high a frequency for human ears to hear. Some bats make the sound with their mouths, while others make it with their nose!

I STILL DON'T LIKE BATS.

THAT'S OK, I THINK YOU SCARED THEM AWAY ANYWAY.

rumble rumble

IS IT OVER?

I THINK SO. LET'S GET BACK TO CAMP.

BRAELIN, DO YOU KNOW WHERE WE ARE?

I DON'T RECOGNIZE ANYTHING. I THINK WE MIGHT BE...

LOST!

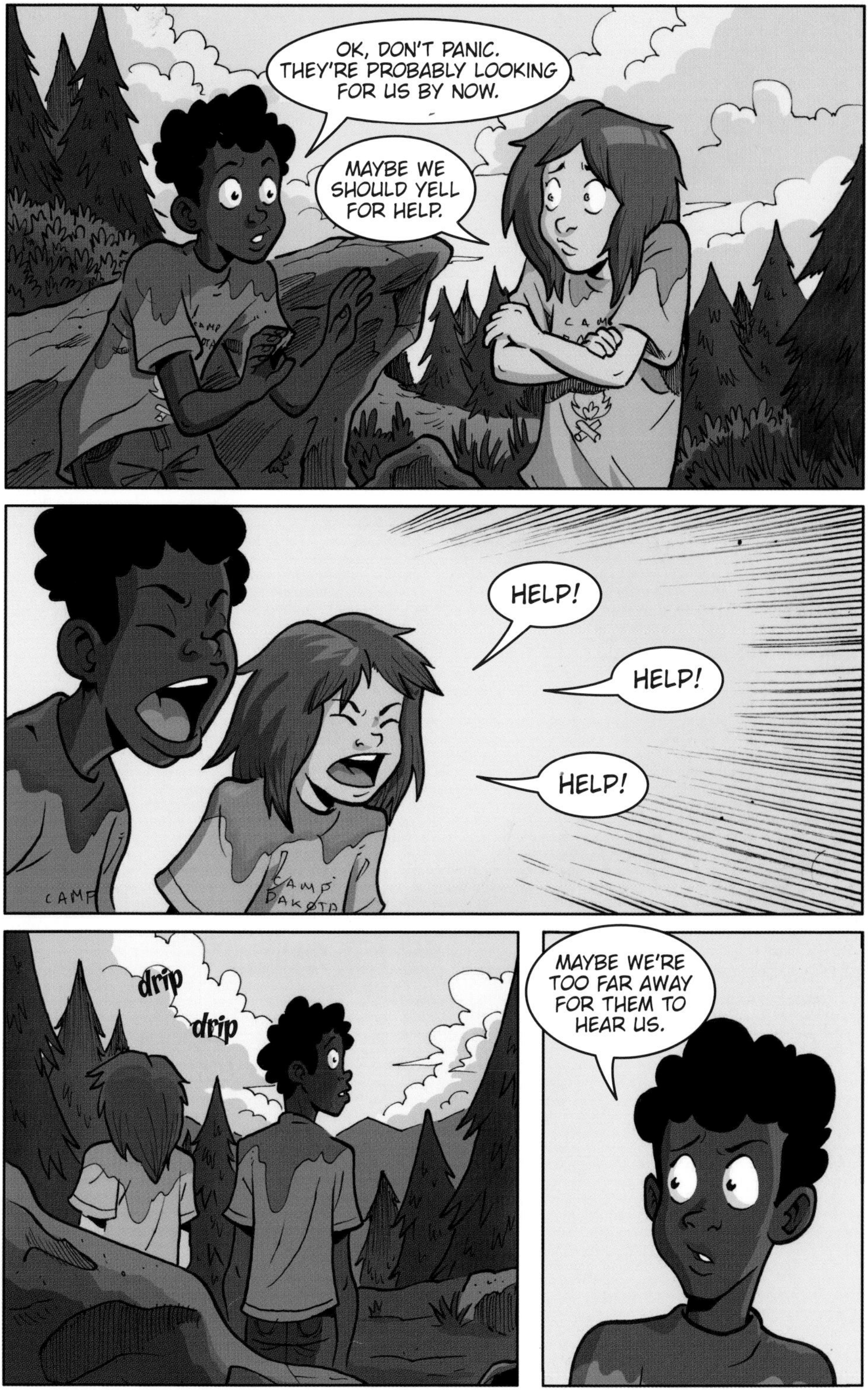
OK, DON'T PANIC. THEY'RE PROBABLY LOOKING FOR US BY NOW.
MAYBE WE SHOULD YELL FOR HELP.
HELP!
HELP!
HELP!
drip
drip
MAYBE WE'RE TOO FAR AWAY FOR THEM TO HEAR US.

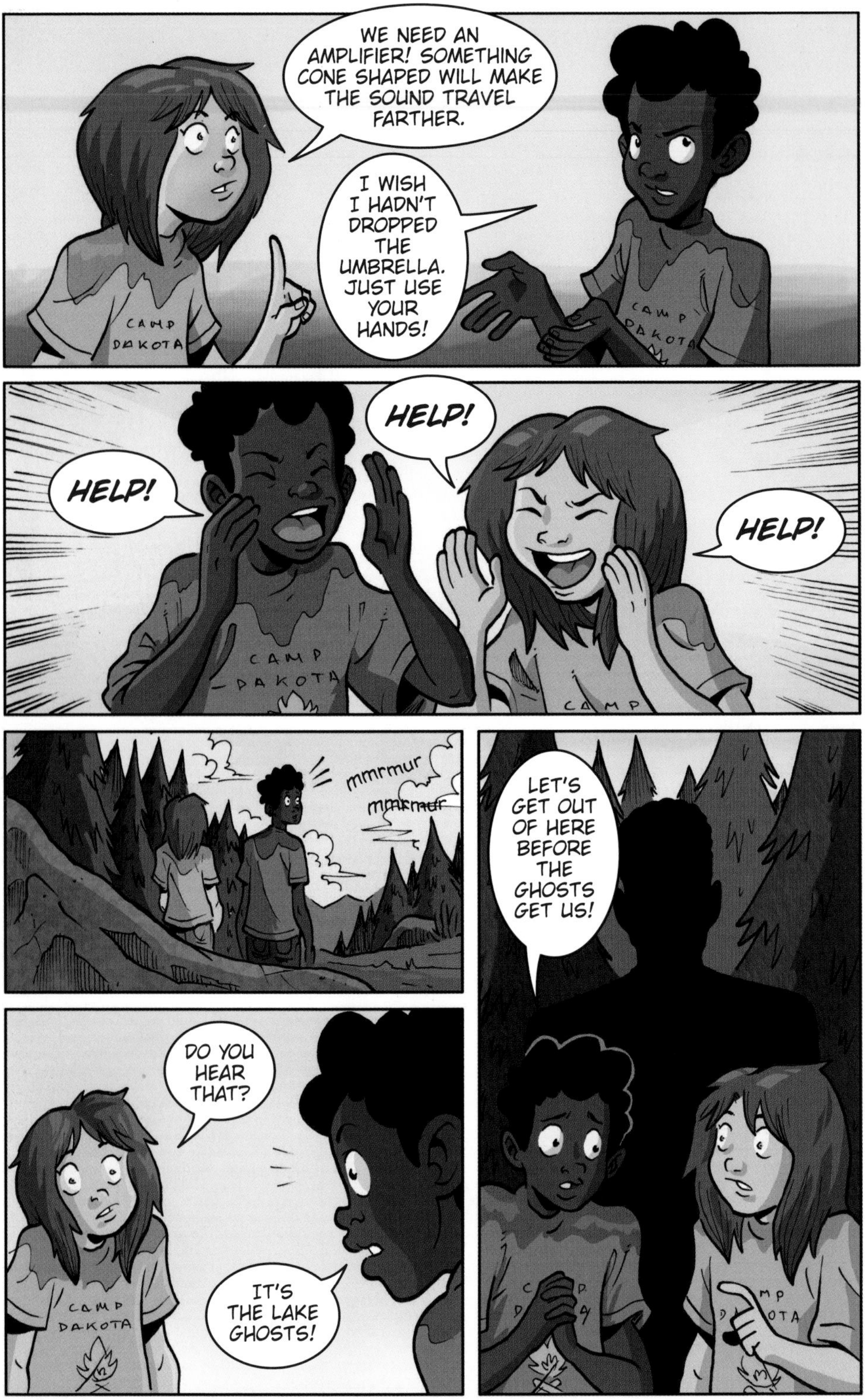
WE NEED AN AMPLIFIER! SOMETHING CONE SHAPED WILL MAKE THE SOUND TRAVEL FARTHER.
I WISH I HADN'T DROPPED THE UMBRELLA. JUST USE YOUR HANDS!
HELP!
HELP!
HELP!
mmrmur
mmrmur
DO YOU HEAR THAT?
IT'S THE LAKE GHOSTS!
LET'S GET OUT OF HERE BEFORE THE GHOSTS GET US!

ARE YOU MEGAN AND BRAELIN?

PINE RIDGE

AAAAH!

YIIIII!

IT'S OK--I'M HERE TO HELP! I'M TYLER, A COUNSELOR FROM CAMP PINE RIDGE.

KYLE CALLED AND ASKED ME TO KEEP AN EYE OUT FOR YOU.

CAMP PINE RIDGE?

CAMP DAKOTA

YEP, ON THE OTHER SIDE OF THE LAKE FROM CAMP DAKOTA.

PINE RIDGE

KYLE? I FOUND THEM.

OK.

HERE. HE WANTS TO TALK TO YOU.

BRAELIN, ARE YOU OK?! IS MEGAN ALL RIGHT?!

KYLE

0:0:30

YEAH, WE'RE OK.

GOOD. GO WITH TYLER TO CAMP PINE RIDGE. WE'LL PICK YOU UP THERE.

YOU'RE THE GHOSTS!

WHAT?

WE AREN'T GHOSTS!

THE KIDS KEPT HEARING VOICES AND THOUGHT THERE WERE GHOSTS, BUT WE FIGURED OUT THAT IT WAS JUST NOISES COMING ACROSS THE LAKE FROM YOUR CAMP.

SO THE VOICES WE HEARD WERE JUST YOU GUYS?

THAT'S RIGHT.

KYLE!

BUT WHY COULDN'T WE HEAR THEM ALL THE TIME?

HMM. WHEN DID YOU HEAR THEM?

I ONLY HEARD THEM AFTER IT RAINED.

AHA! REMEMBER WHAT I TOLD YOU ABOUT THE SPEED OF SOUND AND HOW IT CHANGES IN CERTAIN CONDITIONS?

YOU SAID SOUND TRAVELS FASTER AND FARTHER IN WATER...

AND THERE'S PLENTY OF WATER STILL IN THE AIR AFTER IT RAINS!

SO THE MOIST AIR MADE THE VOICES TRAVEL FARTHER THAN USUAL.

SPEAKING OF TRAVELING-- HOW DID YOU TWO END UP ALONE IN THE WOODS?

WE WERE LOOKING FOR... GHOSTS?

NEXT TIME TRY HUNTING GHOSTS IN THE KITCHEN. YOU BOTH HAVE DISHWASHING DUTY FOR THE WEEK.

KYLE... WE LOST LORAINE'S RECORDER TOO.

I THINK YOU TWO OWE HER A BIG APOLOGY.

SO IT TURNS OUT, THE LAKE GHOSTS ARE REALLY JUST OTHER KIDS, LIKE US.

AND THEY THOUGHT *WE* WERE THE GHOSTS?

YEP.

SEE? I *TOLD* YOU YOU'RE SCARY!

HA HA HA HA HA

Experiments

Try these fun experiments at home or in your classroom.
Make sure you have an adult help you.

Sound Cannon

You will need: cardboard tube from a paper towel roll, plastic wrap,
tape, bowl, rice or small beads, rubber band

1) Cover both ends of the cardboard tube with
plastic wrap, and use the tape to make sure
it stays in place. Make a small hole in the
plastic on one end.

2) Cover an empty bowl tightly with more plastic
wrap. Secure it with the rubber band. Sprinkle
the rice or beads on top of the plastic wrap.

3) Hold the cardboard tube above the bowl, with
the hole end pointing down. Lightly tap the plastic
on the other end of the tube.

What happened?

When you tapped on the plastic covering the tube, the vibration created a
sound wave. The sound wave then hit the plastic on the bowl, which made it
vibrate too. That vibration made the objects resting on top of the plastic move.

Make Your Own Telephone

You will need: 2 empty soup cans with one end removed, about 5 feet of string, 2 people

1) Have an adult use a hammer and a nail to punch a hole in the end of each can.

2) Push the end of the string through the hole from the outside. Then tie a knot in it so it stays attached to the can. Then do the same with the other end of the string and the other can.

3) Have someone take a can and walk away from you until the string is taut. While keeping the string tight, whisper into the open end of the can, while the other person holds the can up to his or her ear.

What Happened?

You created a sound wave when you whispered into the first can. The solid walls of the can collect and concentrate the sound wave. This creates a vibration that travels through the string to the second can. The solid walls of the second can amplify the sound wave that travels through the string.

Mysterious Words

air pressure: the force exerted on a surface by the weight of the air above that surface

amplifier: a device that makes sounds louder, by either condensing or increasing sound waves

atmosphere: a mixture of gases that surround a planetary body, such as Earth

echo: a sound caused by the reflection of sound waves from a surface

echolocation: a way of locating an object by emitting sound and sensing the reflection of the sound from the object

sonar: a system of transmitting a sound wave underwater and using the reflected sound wave to locate objects

sound wave: a type of pressure wave caused by the vibration of an object

vibration: the action of something moving back and forth rapidly.

Could YOU have solved the Mystery of the Whispering Lake Ghosts?

Good thing the kids of Camp Dakota knew a bit about sound—and got some helpful tips from the counselors. See if you caught all the facts they put to use.

- How fast a sound wave travels depends on what it's moving through. Sound travels faster through water than it does through air. When the air is moist, sound can travel farther before it becomes too quiet to hear.

- Cone-shaped amplifiers help concentrate and direct sound waves, so they can travel farther. A megaphone or even your cupped hands can make sounds easier to hear.

- An echo happens when sound waves hit an object and are reflected back in the direction they came from. Bats listen to these echoes to determine the size, shape, and distance of objects near them, even in complete darkness.

THE AUTHOR

LYNDA BEAUREGARD wrote her first story when she was seven years old and hasn't stopped writing since. She also likes teaching kids how to swim, designing websites, directing race cars out onto the track, and throwing bouncy balls for her cat, Becca. She lives near Detroit, Michigan, with her two lovely daughters, who are doing their best to turn her hair gray.

THE ARTIST

GERMAN TORRES has always loved to draw. He also likes to drive his van to the mountains and enjoy a little fresh air with his girlfriend and dogs. But what he really loves is traveling. He lives in a town near Barcelona, Spain, away from the noise of the city.